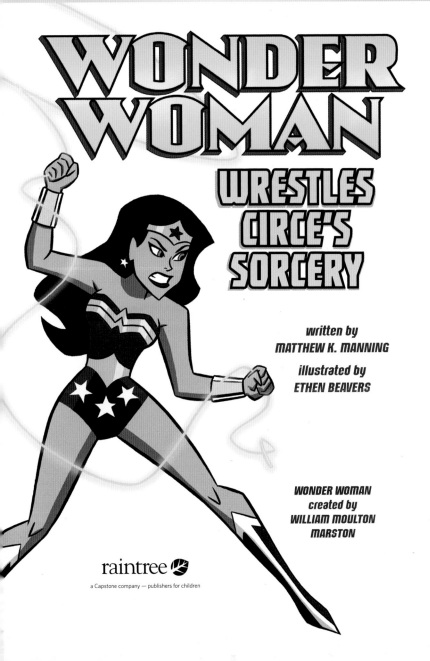

WONDER WOMAN
WRESTLES CIRCE'S SORCERY

written by
MATTHEW K. MANNING

illustrated by
ETHEN BEAVERS

**WONDER WOMAN
created by
WILLIAM MOULTON
MARSTON**

raintree

a Capstone company — publishers for children

Raintree is an imprint of Capstone Global Library Limited,
a company incorporated in England and Wales having its
registered office at 7 Pilgrim Street, London, EC4V 6LB –
Registered company number: 6695582

www.raintree.co.uk
myorders@raintree.co.uk

STAR38696

Applications for the copyright owner's written
permission should be addressed to the
publisher.

Editor: Anna Butzer
Art Director: Bob Lentz
Graphic Designer: Hilary Wacholz

ISBN 978 1 4747 3749 4
21 20 19 18 17
10 9 8 7 6 5 4 3 2 1

British Library Cataloguing in Publication Data
A full catalogue record for this book is available
from the British Library.

Printed in China.

Contents

REAL NAME: Diana of Themyscira/Diana Prince

ROLE: Super hero and government agent

BASE: Gateway City

HEIGHT: 1.83m (6' 0")

EYES: Blue

HAIR: Black

ABILITIES: A master of armed and unarmed combat. Possesses super-strength, super-speed and a Golden Lasso that forces anyone caught in its grasp to speak only the truth.

BACKGROUND: Wonder Woman is Princess Diana of the Amazon island Themyscira. She is the daughter of Queen Hippolyta. Wonder Woman was granted her powers by the Greek gods. She has used those powers to face many different enemies. Some of her enemies are Greek gods and others want to hurt the environment.

CHAPTER 1

THE JUNGLE PARTS

A low hum fills the air. It is so quiet, only the nearby forest animals think to react. They scurry away into their burrows. They dive into the thick foliage of the jungle. The wild grass parts. The leaves of the many nearby trees blow in a wind from some unseen source. Yet there is nothing there. Nothing at all.

When the door in the sky opens, it all makes sense. The Invisible Jet has come to a stop on this remote tropical island. It carries only one passenger . . .

Wonder Woman!

The overgrowth is thick, but Wonder Woman's sword is sharp. She cuts through the vines as if they were paper. With little effort, she slices her way through the jungle. She is used to this landscape, however. The island where she grew up was thick with wild plants.

For Wonder Woman, coming to this place today is almost like coming home.

Finally, she is standing near the centre of the island by a tranquil, quiet pond. The air is silent. No birds are chirping. There is no rustling of small living things in the bushes.

Wonder Woman furrows her brow. Something is definitely wrong. And she knows why.

"I know you're here, Circe," Wonder Woman says. Her voice is calm but stern. "Show yourself."

There is no answer. Wonder Woman looks into the pond. Her eyes narrow as she stares into the water.

And her reflection . . .

. . . changes. Suddenly, it is the sorceress Circe staring back at her.

POOF!

A puff of purple smoke plumes behind
Wonder Woman. She turns, her fists raised.
There stands Circe, a sorceress as powerful
as any Wonder Woman has known.

"You found me a bit quicker than I'd
anticipated," says Circe. "Don't tell me
you're still mad that I changed those
museum guards to pigs?"

"You're coming back to Gateway City," says Wonder Woman. "You'll change those men back, and you'll return the necklace you stole."

"Huh," says Circe. She looks down at the sparkling pendant around her neck. "No, I rather like it."

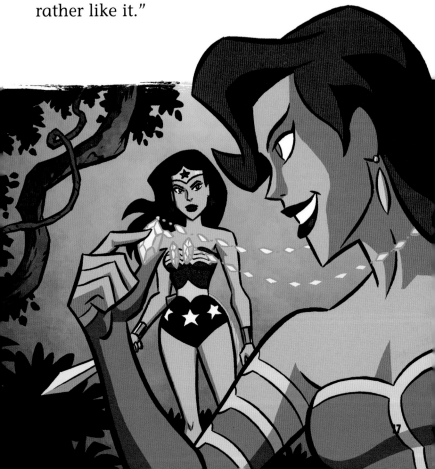

CHAPTER 2

THE PECULIAR PORTAL

Wonder Woman reaches for her magic lasso at her hip.

"Well, I'd like to say that this has been memorable," Circe says. "But honestly, I doubt I'll dwell on it much." Circe waves her hands in the air above her.

A large portal appears behind the sorceress. In one quick movement, she is gone.

Without pause, Wonder Woman leaps after her foe. But the other side of the portal is something far different from a remote tropical island. In fact, it's far different from anything Wonder Woman has ever seen before.

The very nature of reality is different here. Clusters of impossible shapes and colours pass by, floating in something that couldn't even be described as air. Wonder Woman can see Circe escaping into the distance. But her senses are failing her. She doesn't even know which way to go. Her mind races to figure out a way to capture her enemy.

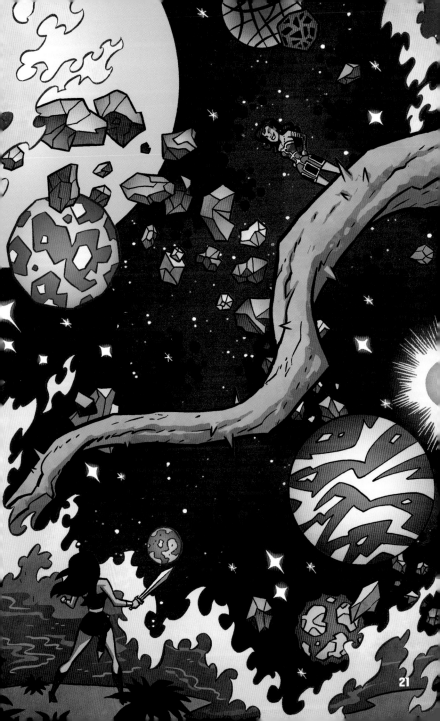

CHAPTER 3

THE HERO IS FORGED

Almost against her will, Wonder Woman's thoughts drift back to years ago. Before she was called Wonder Woman by the world, she was called Diana. She was the Amazon princess of her former home, the uncharted island of Themyscira.

Diana loved her mother Hippolyta, and she loved her Amazon friends. But she had a personality too big for a small, enchanted piece of land. She wanted to explore the outside world. She wanted to do something more with her life.

However, her mother wanted just the opposite. Whenever Diana would ask about places beyond Themyscira's shores, Hippolyta would become silent. She knew the true dangers of the world. And to her, they outweighed its beauty. Above all else, Hippolyta refused to put her daughter in harm's way.

Then came the competition. Diana's mother was the Queen of the Amazons. As such, she decided that one of their number would head to the outside world to serve as ambassador to Themyscira. To choose a worthy representative, a contest was to be held.

It would be an impressive affair. There would be trial by combat. There would be foot races. There would be battles of wits. It would be a long and gruelling process. Only the strong could possibly hope to triumph.

Hippolyta didn't want her daughter entering the competition. But Diana's mind was made up. This was her chance to explore the land beyond their island's shores. So she hid her face and entered the contest.

And she won.

Despite her feelings on the matter, Hippolyta kept her word. Diana was given the mantle of Wonder Woman, and permission to travel to the outside world.

It was what she had always wanted. But deep inside she also felt uneasy.

"I've finally achieved my dream to see the outside world," she said to herself. "Why do I feel so nervous about leaving?"

The outside world was huge. It was disorienting. It was overwhelming. But Diana met every challenge head on with a smile on her face and determination in her eyes. From the Greek god Ares to the ever clever Cheetah, she has faced every problem as a true Wonder Woman.

If she had done it once, she can most certainly do it again.

CHAPTER 4

THE BATTLE RAGES

Wonder Woman's thoughts of the past fade away. She once again takes in her bizarre surroundings. She crouches down and leaps towards Circe. But she ends up jumping to the side, missing the sorceress completely.

Everything Wonder Woman's eyes are telling her seems to be a lie. But she is not fazed. Diana has always had a way of getting to the truth.

Wonder Woman leaps towards Circe again. She misses, but she's closer than before. It is almost as if she's beginning to understand this strange new world around her.

Circe sighs. "You are persistent, aren't you, Amazon?"

Wonder Woman doesn't answer. She concentrates on Circe's voice. She jumps again. She lands on a strange shape, closer still to the sorceress.

"Fine," says Circe. She raises her hands into the air above her. "Let's get this over with."

Circe's eyes turn a dark shade of purple as she speaks an ancient language even Wonder Woman doesn't recognize.

A violent wind blows Wonder Woman backwards. This is the first she's noticed the wind in this weird place. She hadn't thought about it, but the air had been oddly calm. But now, at Circe's command, everything is moving.

Objects and shapes Wonder Woman has never seen before are being drawn to her. It is as if she is a magnet attracting everything around her.

"How do you like it, Wonder Woman?" says Circe. She stands unmoved, unaffected by her spell. "Being the centre of attention?"

"Hm, I'm not crazy about being the centre of attention," Wonder Woman replies. "I'm aiming for quiet confidence."

Wonder Woman throws her lasso at Circe. It misses by a wide length. As she dodges objects she can't fully comprehend, she falls farther away from the sorceress. This world is so strange, so new. But so was the world outside of Themyscira. Diana wasn't prepared for that life. But Wonder Woman was.

Circe looks back over her shoulder and gives Wonder Woman a taunting wink.

"Let's not do this again," she says with a smile.

"Fine by me," Wonder Woman whispers to herself. Then she purses her lips and whistles.

FWEEET!

The nose of the Invisible Jet pierces through the portal. The jet's engine remains quiet, even in this place. As it passes her, Wonder Woman manages to toss her lasso around its nose. She tightens her grip, and lets the jet's automatic pilot do its job.

Circe barely has time to turn around before she sees Wonder Woman's boot flying towards her face.

KABAM!

This dimension might have played havoc on Diana's senses, but it made little difference to her Invisible Jet's onboard computer.

CHAPTER 5

THE WINNING WOMAN

Circe doesn't wake as Wonder Woman binds her in her magic lasso. Wonder Woman removes the stolen necklace from around Circe's neck. The sorceress doesn't stir as Diana places her in the back of her Invisible Jet. Wonder Woman hops into the cockpit and races back to Gateway City.

When she arrives at the heart of the city, Wonder Woman swoops down in front of the Gateway City Police Department. Circe only lets out the faintest whimper as Wonder Woman drops her on the front steps. Standing over the defeated sorceress are a police officer, an animal control officer and two pigs.

"Here's the necklace Circe took from the museum," says Wonder Woman as she hands the stolen jewellery to the police officer. "And the power of my lasso will force her to change those museum guards back into men."

"We can't thank you enough," replies the police officer.

With a wave farewell, Wonder Woman returns to her Invisible Jet. Then she fires up its engines and soars into the sky.

Over the Gateway City Bridge, a doorway opens in the sky. Those who notice see the figure of a woman leaping from it. Some may even be close enough to see the smile on her face. The smile of . . .

Wonder Woman!

CIRCE

REAL NAME: Circe

ROLE: Greek goddess and sorceress

BASE: Aeaea

HEIGHT: 1.80m (5' 11")

EYES: Red

HAIR: Purple

ABILITIES: Possesses nearly limitless magical power, including the power to transform mortal beings into animals and the power to project her voice, image and energy bolts over long distances. She can also manipulate reality, fire destructive magical energy blasts and teleport between dimensions.

BACKGROUND: Circe is an immortal sorceress who spends the majority of her time on the island of Aeaea. Circe uses a special plant that grows on this island to make an elixir called vitae. This elixir allows Circe to stay eternally youthful and beautiful. Circe's wide variety of magical abilities make her an extremely dangerous foe.

Wonder Woman's magical bracelets are the perfect defence against Circe's magical attacks. They allow Wonder Woman to block magic, preventing damage or transformation.

Circe loves nothing more than humiliating others. She also loves turning human beings into animals.

GLOSSARY

ambassador person sent by a government to represent it in another country

bizarre very unusual or strange

faze to cause someone to feel afraid or uncertain

foe enemy

furrow deep wrinkle; someone might furrow their brow when they are annoyed or confused

havoc great damage and chaos

plume something that rises into the air in a tall, thin shape

stern strict or harsh

uncharted unknown territory; not on any map

About the author

Matthew K. Manning is the author of over 50 books. He has contributed to many comic books as well, including *Teenage Mutant Ninja Turtles: Amazing Adventures*, *Beware the Batman* and the crossover miniseries *Batman/TMNT Adventures*. He currently resides in Asheville, North Carolina, USA, with his wife Dorothy and their two daughters, Lillian and Gwendolyn. Visit him online at www.matthewkmanning.com.

About the illustrator

Ethen Beavers is a professional comic book artist from Modesto, California, USA. His best-known works for DC Comics include *Justice League Unlimited* and *Legion of Superheroes in the 31st Century*. He has also illustrated for other top publishers, including Marvel, Dark Horse and Abrams.

WRITING PROMPTS

1. Diana entered the competition to be chosen as the ambassador to Themyscira even though her mother said she couldn't. When, if ever, is it okay to break the rules?

2. If you had Wonder Woman's Invisible Jet what would you do with it? Where would you go? Who would you see? Write about it.

3. If you could have any ability or tool that Circe or Wonder Woman use in this book, which would you choose? What would you use it for? Write about it.

DISCUSSION QUESTIONS

1. Which of Wonder Woman's abilities or magical items helped her the most in this book? Why?

2. Wonder Woman is overwhelmed when she travels to a strange, new place. Have you ever felt that way when travelling somewhere you've never been?

3. This book uses illustrations to help tell the story. Which one do you think helps the reader understand the action the most? Why?

READ THEM ALL

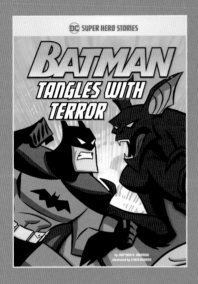

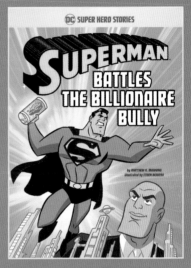